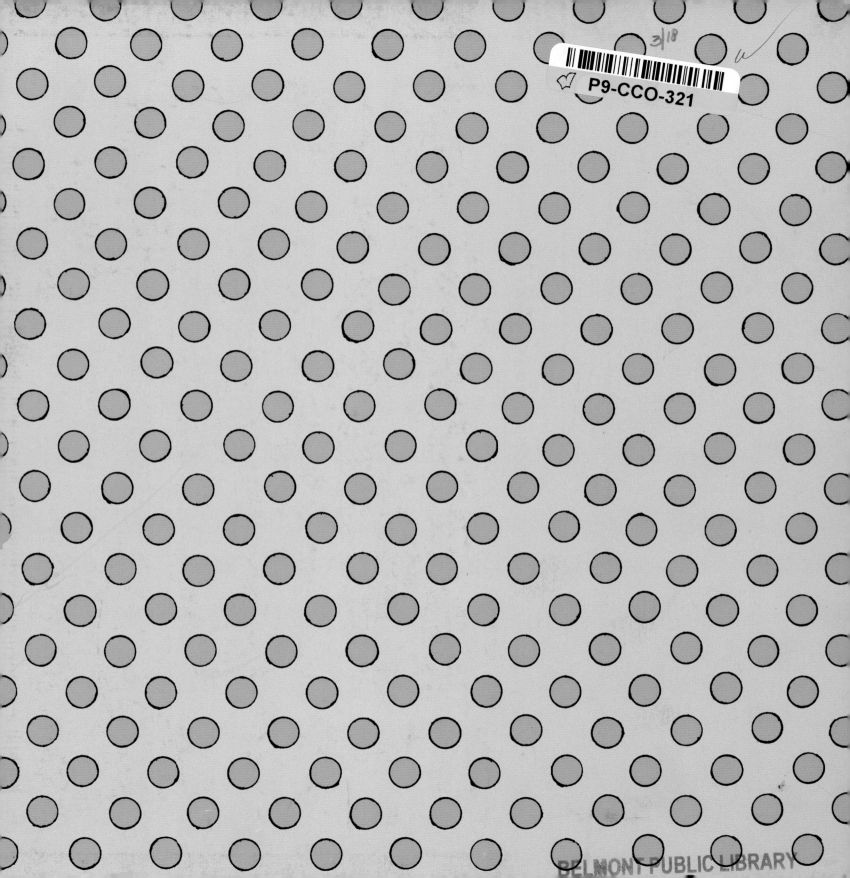

# Lots more animals should definitely <u>not</u> wear clothing.

written by Judi Barrett
and drawn by Ron Barrett

atheneum

A CAITLYN DLOUHY BOOK
Atheneum Books for Young Readers
New York   London   Toronto   Sydney   New Delhi

To my dear friend Joan—J. B.

To my grand grandson, Søren—R. B.

**ATHENEUM BOOKS FOR YOUNG READERS**
An imprint of Simon & Schuster Children's Publishing Division
1230 Avenue of the Americas, New York, New York 10020
Text copyright © 2018 by Judi Barrett
Illustrations copyright © 2018 by Ron Barrett
All rights reserved, including the right of reproduction in whole or in part in any form.
**ATHENEUM BOOKS FOR YOUNG READERS** is a registered trademark of Simon & Schuster,
Inc. Atheneum logo is a trademark of Simon & Schuster, Inc.
For information about special discounts for bulk purchases, please contact Simon & Schuster
Special Sales at 1-866-506-1949 or business@simonandschuster.com.
The Simon & Schuster Speakers Bureau can bring authors to your live event. For more
information or to book an event, contact the Simon & Schuster Speakers Bureau at
1-866-248-3049 or visit our website at www.simonspeakers.com.
Book design by Ron Barrett and Lauren Rille
The text for this book was set in Futura.
The illustrations for this book were rendered in pen and ink with digital color.
Manufactured in China
1217 SCP
First Edition
10  9  8  7  6  5  4  3  2  1
CIP data for this book is available from the Library of Congress.
ISBN 978-1-4814-8866-2
ISBN 978-1-4814-8867-9 (eBook)

# Animals should definitely <u>not</u> wear clothing . . .

because
it would hamper
a horse,

**because
a frog might
jump out of it,**

because
it would be
unbearable
for a bear,

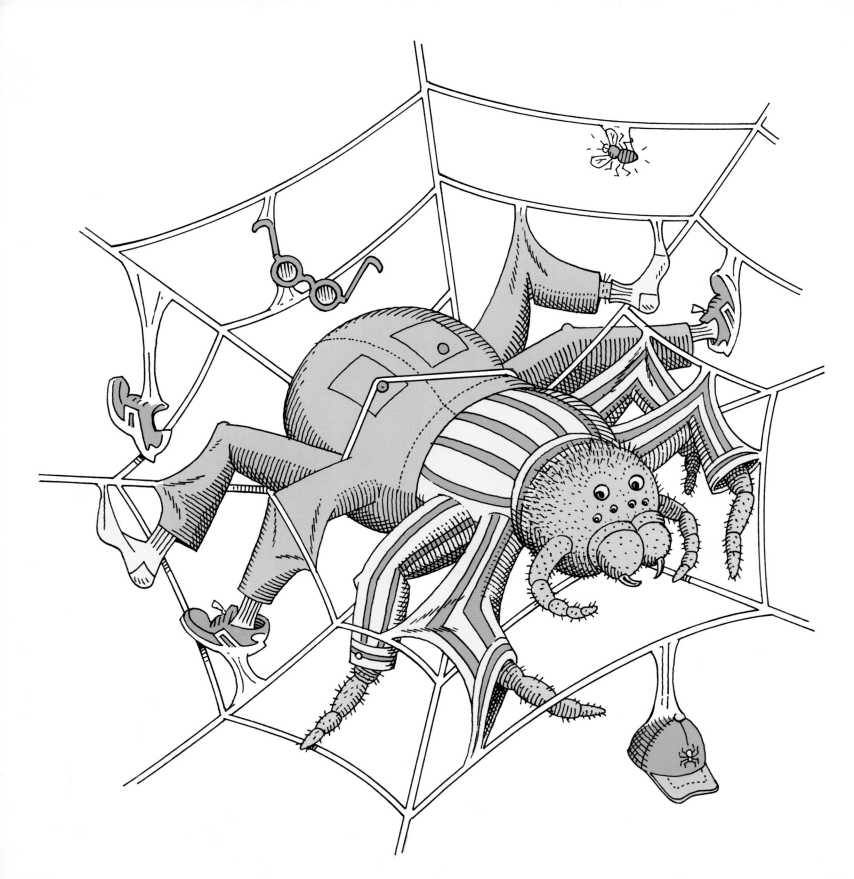

because
a spider could
get tangled,

because
it would be
foolish for
a fish,

because
an elk would
have too many
choices,

because
a crab would
tear it up,

because
a turtle
has a turtleneck
of its own,

because
a penguin is
already dressed,

because
a skunk could
make it stinky,

because
it would fluster
a flamingo,

because
a hyena
might find it
hilarious,

because
it could
overwhelm
a caterpillar,

and most of all,
because
it would be
absurd for
an armadillo.

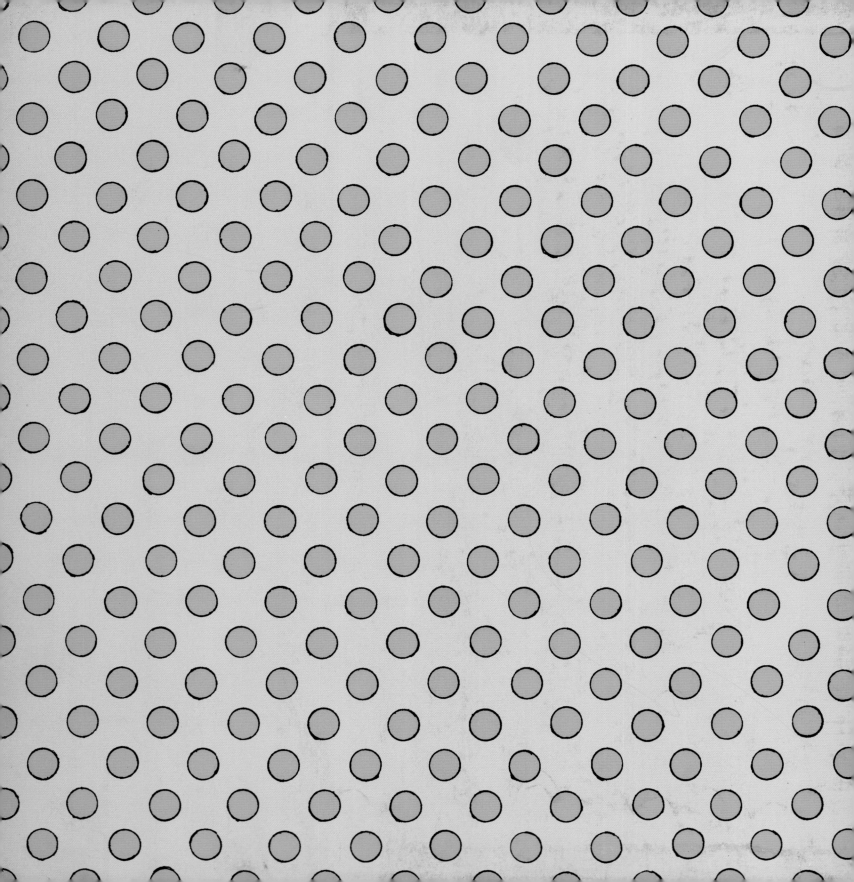